The Fabulous Dead

by

Andriana Minou

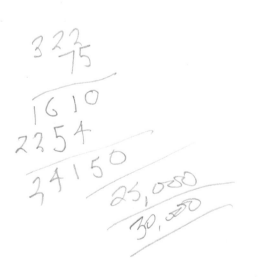

KERNPUNKT • PRESS

Art: Cover and interior illustrations by Andriana Minou
Book Design: Jesi Buell

Permissions:
Nietzsche's quote from Kritische Studienausgabe, published with kind permission of Rowman & Littlefield

C.G. Jung's quotes from The Red Book (edited by Sonu Shamdasani) published with kind permission of W.W. Norton

1st Printing: 2020

ISBN-13 978-1-7323251-6-6

KERNPUNKT Press
Hamilton, New York 13346

Table of Contents

List of Illustrations

(in order of appearance)

Cover: The Fabulous Dead (Chinese ink)

She eats like a bird (pencil sketch)

Escaping Titian (pastels)

Salva me ab ore leonis (pencil sketch)

A cage went looking for a bird (ink sketch)

Marlene raised on turnips and potatoes (pencil sketch)

Tea(r)time (pencil sketch)

Memoirs of a goldfish (pastels)

Practice makes perfect (pencil sketch)

The Skyscraper Queen in Rumours Motel

I live the life of another. In Rumours Motel, I am dressed as a skyscraper queen, my shoulders draped in a shawl of stars and fog, while I'm scraping the edge of the night sky with my pinkie nail, peeking, turning my nose upwards, searching for the smell of creatures never to be seen. I am amongst them; I, living the life of another.

The fabulous dead are like dust. They sneak into everything. And the more you dust, the more they spread and merge with each other and change shapes and cover everything and creep inside your nostrils and then into your lungs and then into your blood, under your skin, until all mirrors reflect only their faces.

The fabulous dead speak incessantly but have no voice. After all, that's what death is—something articulated in the void. A rather unremarkable repetition. A moment escaping, behind a turned back. An abrupt emptiness. Their mouths are dry and their skin is numb. They don't kiss, they don't caress. They just speak to me incessantly and I see their lips move with emphatic indolence.

In Rumours Motel tonight, I am dressed as a skyscraper queen. Yesterday I was a blasphemous astronomer, the day after tomorrow I'll be a sweet-voiced chimney-sweep, last week I was a loquacious taxi driver, a suicidal author, a kind-hearted whore, and next month I'll be a melancholy housewife, a corrupt bishop, an autistic superhero. It is such a relief, not being obliged to live your own life, simply letting yourself rely on someone else's choices. I feel so carefree when I spend the night here, a puppet in the hands of someone I have invented in order to be invented by them. Because living is no laughing matter. Who bears to drag this body, further weighed down by every fragment of self on top of it, until the end? Who has the patience to assemble this dreadfully clockwork chaos? Inhale, exhale, inhale, exhale, and the responsibility keeps growing, the responsibility to find how you want to live, to urgently become who you have to be in order to live. Perhaps, to become yet another fabulous dead.

In Rumours Motel, people come in order to live someone else's life. They come to be what others think of them, to become impressions of themselves. Then, when they grow tired of disguises invented by others, they may choose the life of anyone they like.

Even their own life.

Three Breaths[1]

Coming home yesterday afternoon, I found in my garden Virginia with rocks in her pockets, Sarah with shoelaces around her neck, and Sylvia with the oven on her head. They were playing cards and gossiping. Their chatter was lovely. They were discussing breathing. *Breathing is the root of all evil,* they said, and they all agreed. Sylvia merely nodded because the oven covered her entire head and no one could hear her anyway. *Breathing is the root of all evil,* they said, *all this repetition, a lifetime wasted breathing, it's inconceivable, such pity, oh my, oh my, how sad.* I sat next to them on a low stool and I served the Bloody Marys. The three ladies were delighted, especially Sarah who needed a tonic.

I haven't slept in 18 years, she remarked playing absentmindedly with the shoelaces around her neck, and Sylvia laughed from inside the oven, while Virginia's eyes widened.

---

[1] Virginia Woolf drowned herself in the Thames after putting stones in her pockets. Sarah Kane hung herself with her shoelaces. Sylvia Plath killed herself by putting her head in a gas oven.

Days in London dawn early in June. First, the birds start chirping in the garden and then the morning light wakes me. I hired a handyman to put some blinds up but he hasn't turned up in 18 years.

Sylvia's muffled giggle resonated again from inside the oven. Virginia kept caressing the rocks in her pocket, and took another sip from her drink. Then, she smiled awkwardly at me, her teeth red from the tomato juice.

Could you please pass me the pepper? she enquired. *I need more pepper. I love pepper. It makes me sneeze. I love sneezing. It is like reverse breathing. Rumour has it that while sneezing one's soul escapes through the nose and as it's floating unprotected in the air, it may get snatched. All that only because of a single peppercorn. And what about you, miss? You have abstained from this conversation until now,* she told me, her teeth red.

Indeed, tell us, what do you think about breathing? added Sarah, and Sylvia purred with pleasure.

For a petit little moment every once in a while, a moment so tiny that it is invisible to the naked eye, inaudible to the naked ear, and odourless to the naked nose, leaving only a trace of fresh rust on my naked brain, every once in a while, as I was saying, I don't remember who I am, I cannot recall my name and what I look like, for a split second this inquisitive drone scrutinising incessantly what I am, what my name is, and how I look, becomes suspended, irresponsive, without the affirmative response that repeats my name like a silent incantation that lulls reassuringly, and so the flow of this word is interrupted and it is as if the planets freeze momentarily in place, also evident from the fact that the stars too cease their flickering song, all of nature's creatures lift their heads in awe, and the wind won't whistle, nor sun shine so bright, and I myself first grope my body nervously searching for my umbilical cord in terror, and then my arms drop into space and I greedily inhale my favourite food, the most savoury aetheric delicacy, a freedom yet unnamed, that of silence.

Sarah removed the oven from her head. Her beauty took our breath away. *Let's drink to that*, she said, raising her glass.

"Beauty killed the Brahms"[2]

Brahms put down the receiver violently. He rushed to the kitchen and opened a jar of sauerkraut. Only sauerkraut could calm him down. He always used a tiny silver fork to eat it and he let the juices drip down his beard all the way to his potbelly. As a young man, he used to be very lean, almost cachectic, and his voice was high-pitched. Girls used to mock him, in spite of his excellent piano playing, a talent that usually appeals to the opposite sex. At least he didn't wear glasses too. By the time he turned twenty-two, every night he would dream that he was King Kong. Between his thumb and index finger, he was holding a half-naked blonde from the waist; he was growling sweet nothings in her ear while everyone else was watching in awe, tufts of garlands and confetti gushing out of their wide-open mouths. Rumour has it that he had an affair with his best friend's wife, Clara. The truth is he was in love

---

[2] See the closing lines of the 1933 movie *King Kong*

with her, but no more than with all the rest. All Clara wanted was to feed him fruit puree. Then she would take him in her arms, but only until he had digested. Brahms hated fruit puree. After their dates, he would get back home in tears and devour sauerkraut, struggling to eliminate that sickly sweet taste from his palate.

In his thirties, he finally started getting fat and hairy all over. It was extremely fulfilling. Girls still mocked him, now calling him King Kong, no matter how many ballads he would play for them on the piano. That was when Brahms decided to invent the telephone. He installed a telephone right on his desk, where he used to spend most of his day composing. The view of the telephone filled him with infinite peace. He didn't feel lonely any more. That was inexplicable, of course, as he was perfectly aware of the fact that not another soul in the world was in possession of a telephone device, since it was still only 1863, therefore he also knew that there was no chance whatsoever that his phone would ring. But he had no intention of analysing the inner peace offered to him by this device, regardless of its absurdity. Since he had invented the telephone, the fact that girls didn't fancy him didn't concern him at all. Nor did he feel compelled to try and become attractive to them in any way. For twenty years he dedicated himself to his music, composing night and day, as if a part of his brain was still convinced that if a girl fancied him, she could always just give him a ring.

Things had changed during the past week, though. Every morning at eleven o'clock sharp, that is, the exact moment he had started composing and was at the point when he had shut out all external stimuli, blissfully floating amongst his deliciously euphoric neurons, the inexplicable happened. The telephone started ringing. The first time, he thought there must have been something wrong with the mechanism. So he let it ring and just kept composing. After he had finished with his sonata, he fetched his tools, opened up the device and checked if there were any broken cogs or cables in there. Everything seemed in perfect order. The second day, he gaped at the ringing phone for a while and then picked up the receiver, although he had no clue why. He didn't manage to speak. That would have been too much. At the other end of the line, all he heard was a breathing sound, and then he put down the receiver in terror.

The following days were pure hell. He couldn't focus on his music and kept consuming countless jars of sauerkraut. Even when he pretended he didn't pay any attention to it, the telephone would keep ringing until he'd pick it up. At the other end of the line, that peculiar breathing sound was always there, the sound of someone waiting calmly for something to happen, sooner or later. And on this side of the line, it was always him, unable to convince himself to surrender completely to that absurdity by uttering one single word. Because that's just how Brahms was. He could only endure the absurdities he had created with his own hands. Allowing his absurdity to merge with someone else's absurdity was too transcendental for his nature. He preferred to suspect he was paranoid, rather than step beyond the thin line dividing the reality of others from his own reality. He didn't appreciate any of those two realities. He just wanted to stand precisely on the thin dividing line and keep up appearances, gulping down his sauerkraut.

One day, though, the phone did stop ringing. It was nearly midday and still nothing. Brahms kept picking up the receiver, bringing it to his ear eagerly, realising that the line was dead and putting it down in anger. As time went by, he grew angrier and angrier. He wasn't sure why. He swallowed his sauerkraut greedily, wondering why the possibility of things returning to normal bothered him so. As he brought his tiny silver spoon towards his mouth, he suddenly heard a shrill cry. He looked around him in alarm but soon realised—he was a musician after all—that the strange shriek was coming directly from his fork.

And then he saw her entangled in the sauerkraut he was about to put in his mouth, a tiny half-naked blonde, screaming, struggling to escape from his fork. He caught her waist between his thumb and index finger carefully, and took a closer look at her. Her hair was platinum, her eyebrows extremely thin and she kept screaming intolerably. He looked out of the window and saw hundreds of faces stuck on the windowpane.

Don't be scared, my darling, calm down, Brahms whispered in the woman's ear. But she didn't seem comforted and kept shrieking. Brahms realised that the time of thin dividing lines and kept-up appearances was gone for good.

Don't be afraid, I love you.

Everyone else was watching in awe, tufts of garlands and confetti gushing out of their wide-open mouths.

Gaium Garum Larum

"What? Do you not think that the garum sociorum, this costly extract of poisonous fish, burns up the stomach with its salted putrefaction?"

- Seneca, Letter 95

Julius Caesar is standing jauntily by the sink, gutting fish for his favourite garum sauce[3]. Twenty-three fish is the optimal amount for the preparation of this sauce, which can accompany anything: meat, salads, snacks, tedious lovers, clingy friends, insignificant enemies, but, above all, it assists the dissolution of indigestible doubts. When a nagging suspicion won't let you sleep, eat, think of anything else, or even breathe, an otherwise unnecessary suspicion that, nevertheless, extends its cunning tentacles to strangle your brain, then the garum eases the swallowing and digestion of such thoughts. It also offers relief from the persistent feeling of heartburn that usually follows any attempt at digesting those thoughts in order to achieve some peace of mind.

For his beloved garum, Caesar extracts the guts from 23 different types of small fish, such as smelt, anchovies,

---

[3] Garum: A type of sauce which was prepared in ancient Rome from sundried fish guts and was one of the most popular condiments of ancient Roman cuisine.

13

sprat, and tuna, all of which he eviscerates with artistry and then drops in a small basin in his sink. *Et tu Brute!* he shouts triumphantly with each stab. Oh, the joys of domestic activity. Eyes fixed to meet his victims' empty stare, he grabs the fish cheerfully and guts them with a broad smile. Today's garum will be consumed to cure a silly suspicion that has been tormenting him for the past week. A few nights ago he dreamt that he was blind. Therefore, technically, he didn't see anything suspicious, only, in the darkness of his dream, he hears voices all around him, as if he is in the market; greengrocers, fishmongers, butchers, gossiping housewives, customers haggling, bored men talking about sports. But he doesn't see anything. He only struggles to continue his proud walk between this invisible, tumultuous mob, steering clear of passers-by, minding the stalls, guided by the unnerving voices. It was in this dream that the first fragment of that absurd anxiety, which has been tormenting him recently, was born; nobody must suspect he's blind. His blindness must remain unseen by a crowd who wait for the moment a great man will expose a single fragment of weakness in order to devour him. Caesar keeps walking among them, head high, and he can smell their contempt, oozing like fish guts drying under the sun. The sun is resting on his eyelids yet everything remains dark and, just like this torture of pretending that everything is under control, the market seems endless, and, for the first time in his life, Caesar feels like crying, he feels the tears filling up his blind eyes, but manages to wake up in angst before shedding a single tear. What a nightmare. Men don't cry. Let alone great men, this he knows too well. Fortunately he woke up just in time - the very least expected by a great man, really. But that filthy suspicion still persists, it's been a week now. His hidden weakness, he fears, the weakness he himself has not discovered yet, they will sense it, they who lurk patiently. He's afraid he may not be such a great man after all and they will call him out any minute now, and maybe even 23[4] small fishes are not enough for the digestion of such a great fear.

He is now holding a small mullet in his hands, admiring its red colour. He makes a face imitating the mullet's fat lips and tickles its long barbels. His stare escapes outside the window. A seagull is sitting on a pine tree with a tall and slim trunk. Cutting across the tree's needles, bundled together as if positioned by a giant marble hand at the top of the tree, the seagull's stare meets Casear's. This seagull is vicious, thinks Caesar, and immediately shakes his head lightly to rid his exhausted mind of yet another unfounded suspicion. Eyes back to the mullet in his hands and, all of a sudden, something

---

[4] Julius Caesar was assassinated in 44 BC. He was stabbed 23 times.

miniscule, a single scale, gets in his eye, and Caesar shrieks, drops the mullet back into the sink, falls to the floor, the small basin with the guts after him, he rolls and folds into two, blinded, the scale scratches his eye, it stings, and he struggles to stand up again, but keeps slipping on the fish guts, he reaches out trying to hold on to something, he feels the tears filling up his eyes, just about to sweep away the scale that tortures him in their salty tide, but he refuses to cry because men never cry, let alone great men.

Agapornis[5]

Eat me like candy.
It's spring, and at last
I have no will.

- Rumi

Wittgenstein was measuring his ignorance. The extreme heat always obstructed him, unaccustomed as he was to heat waves. Therefore, in part because of his understandable ignorance of the appropriate measure to measure ignorance, he often lost count. Each time he lost count, he wetted his lips to concentrate, since the residual putrid flavour of the perennial passing of ritual words through them tasted so familiar that it managed to bring him back to order. *What might the cure be?* he thought frantically. *What might the cure be to this bad breath, or rather to this foul taste from which I suffer? Words leave a footprint; how can I erase it?*

---

[5] The Agapornis (ancient Greek for "lovebird") is a type of parrot from Africa. It has a very affectionate disposition, hence its name. It has been observed that this type of bird develops extremely strong bonds with its mate, usually mating for life, and in case one of them dies, the other one soon follows. That is why agapornises are also called "inseparable partners." Some believe that agapornises in captivity should be kept in couples, never to be bought separately. Others believe agapornises can survive without a mate, as long as humans show them a great deal of love and affection. They live for 10-15 years.

17

The dark-skinned, bare-breasted young woman who was in charge of preparing the meal that afternoon started chopping a strange variety of root resembling an exceptionally red carrot straight into the pot. In their fall, the vegetables splashed tepid water on Wittgenstein's face, but he didn't react as his attention was drawn to the small parrot resting on the woman's shoulder, every now and then rubbing its beak affectionately round her neck. *Agapornis*, thought Wittgenstein, *commonly known as "lovebird"; a species of African parrot that mates only once in its lifetime and is reported to spend its days exclusively in amorous play with its partner.* He is itching to ask her about the whereabouts of the partner of the female resting on her shoulder, as it is well known that this species does not survive in solitude, but in the ocean of words filling his brain, Wittgenstein cannot find even one that the young indigenous woman will understand, as she continues chopping vegetables into the pot where he himself is floating. What is most interesting is that this woman appears not to speak any language whatsoever. She does not give a sign of being able to speak in general, not a single word has escaped her lips, and yet she doesn't seem mute or deaf, only silent, like a bird unwilling to sing.

The water's temperature in the pot is rising alarmingly and Wittgenstein, now slightly scorched, abandons his efforts at concentrating. He shuts his eyes and is amazed to see a golden background with a blurry figure forming at the centre of his non-vision. He tightens his eyelids, struggling to maintain this image, vine leaves and forget-me-nots scattering irregularly among the golden background, spirals, circles, squares, and aphrodisiac seaweed entangled around two faces, one of them held between a pair of hands in a high-definition amorous clasp, then two female feet stretching like a set of violin strings ready to sing, and loneliness has forever been wiped off this image. Another pair of hands clasped in fear that the following moment won't resemble this gold-plated fraction of time any more, the other face, half-concealed, half-concealing a kiss and so the whole image, all this gold, is blinding him to reveal at last the secret it guards, the never-decaying ritual of the lips, around two familiar faces; that of the silent cook, and Wittgenstein himself boiling in her pot.

I want you to eat me, he tells her, opening his eyes. *I want you to eat me whole, you yourself, to cook me, to chew me, to swallow me, to digest me piece by piece and all that remains from me, after it has passed through your body, to scatter into the jungle, to be absorbed by the earth, to be captured by the rain, and drunk by the leaves, to rustle in the wind, to be inhaled by the birds, and then a bird to lay an egg out of which an agapornis will hatch, then chirp, and fly, and sit on your shoulder and live there forever, in eternal embrace with your own agapornis, inside a never-ending kiss, reciting secretly next to your ear the cure to the traces of rotting words, and so to live incorruptible within our shared mystery, two agapornises hiding in order to reveal what they hold secret.*

The young woman looks at Wittgenstein with her big eyes but he cannot discern whether she understands him in the least. The female agapornis flies from her shoulder to his shoulder and she reaches to take it back. She brings her face close to the little parrot, as if to kiss its beak and Wittgenstein takes her dark face into his[6] hands in a high-definition enamoured clasp, while her feet are stretching just like a set of violin strings ready to sing. Then, she throws more wood into the fire and leaves with her hands clasped, chirping. Wittgenstein's body is cooking in the pot, and the measure for ignorance is revealed whilst brought to the boil. The traces of all words have been erased.

---

[6] The philosopher, Ludwig Wittgenstein was a devoted fan of the "exotic" singer, Carmen Miranda.

Escaping Titian[7]

Glenn Gould[8] can't get his hands around the organ. Instead of the indulgent, fresh butter-like sound of the Goldberg Variations, his fingers trip as if entangled among Medusa's snake hair. It is irrelevant anyway, since this whole affair is but an excuse to peek between Aphrodite's plump thighs. He is spying as if to find a pill for his high blood pressure, long lost in there. Aphrodite is caressing her thigh absentmindedly, engrossed in the sensation of velvet red on her bare skin, indulging secretly on the soft touch of a frowning cupid who whispers a secret in her ear. Outside the window, a peacock is drinking water out of a faun's hand and a pair of deer are, unbeknownst to them, preparing to mate.

They can't see us. We are escaping them.

Just now we climbed down the wide staircase, you holding me for support. To keep me warm, you have covered

---

[7] See Titian's painting "Venus with an Organist and Cupid"

[8] Glenn Gould (1932-1982) was a Canadian pianist, one of the greatest of the 20th century, especially celebrated for his legendary interpretations of the Goldberg Variations by J.S.Bach.

me with a red cape, a colour known to best cover bareness. We are now among the lean trees with the corroded tree-tops, out in the garden. We can hear the Goldberg Variations dissolving out of the open window, but we don't turn to look back. Throughout the history of humanity, looking back is consistently a bad idea, it exposes our most ingenuous face to the creature lurking behind us.

Aphrodite's inconceivably pale, soft belly resembles softly whisked meringue, about to be mixed with mother's milk and then spilt on the cosmos. This infamous milk over which no one has ever cried, a fact suggesting that even this very Anglo-Saxon stiff upper lip might inexplicably be yet another ancient Greek discovery. In the tempo of a Sarabande, Aphrodite's tummy inflates and deflates, inhaling and exhaling Glenn Gould's enchanting whispers, the deer continue to pose in that monumentally solitary moment immediately before the inevitable glance, the moment before the peacock sees the water passing over hairy arms, the moment before Aphrodite turns her head to witness Glenn Gould peeping at the slit between her legs, this moment we carry in our pockets like a miniscule full moon that will deliver dawn, as we cross the rusty gardens. We won't look back, no one ever looks back. Cheek to cheek, we will cover the distance. We won't look back at all this beautiful noise fading behind us nostalgically. We are headed where the clouds meet the earth. We won't look back, no one can see us. We are escaping.

Underwater

Yet deeper dive, if thou wouldst delight me

- Richard Wagner, *Rheingold*

More often than not, when sitting in solitude, various frightful creatures come into my company: reptiles, insects, sacred and unholy monsters, mythological beasts, and past lovers. It was while I was having coffee at a seaside bar, carefree, when Wagner joined me. He ordered a "Vhiskey" with the awareness that, had he had ordered a "whiskey", he would then have to tolerate being addressed as "Whagner", a thought that would undoubtedly cause him a fit of enraged hysteria. Paradoxically, Wagner was in the mood for talking business, even though it is profoundly obvious to the sufficiently sane that I am probably the least appropriate person for such conversation.

Operas I find tedious alas, he tells me, and also that he'd like to retire in Venice with an eye to start a business selling all sorts of gas. Oxygen for hospitals or for welding, helium for hot-air balloons or for fraternity parties, neon for neon lights

29

or for domestic freezers and so on and so forth. For hours he details all the gasses he could sell and all their prospective uses and, in between, he keeps repeating with a goofy smile that he will be literally trading hot air. It was a scheme as ambitious as all of his operas put together, almost like an opera itself in its elaborate description, though the leitmotiv of hot air I found somewhat silly.

Accustomed as he was to cooler temperatures, Wagner appeared increasingly hot, with miniscule golden drops of sweat covering his temples, while his cheeks and forehead he wiped every now and then with a silk handkerchief, and I could see his skin creasing and spreading like dough denser than the waters of the Rhine—filled as it was with the corpses of the fooled—and his face changed with each touch of the handkerchief until I couldn't bear it anymore. I stuck my eye in his ear and peeked into his brain to see a sea with thousands of English horns, trombones, clarinets, violins, cellos, and bassoons lying on the seabed or floating in the green waters, covered with slime and mould and corals, seaweed, urchins, and small fish swimming in and out of the mouthpieces and the open keys, caressing the strings, spreading bubbles filled with music traveling muted and eternal, and I shiver. I shake with awe from head to toe, yet Wagner continues sipping his whiskey nonchalantly, contracting his lips oddly, like a fish's mouth or a wailing baby wo-ah wo-ah wo-ah. *Mr. Wagner, Mr. Wagner* I whisper, terrified in the thought of bursting one of the beautiful bubbles. *Mr. Wagner music does not grow old, music in our head stays forever young and, as much as we burden it with human baggage, it never gets wrinkled,* and Wagner seems to shake his head in agreement, *indeed my dear how could it ever grow old, this which dies countless times, each note a death rattle, each rest a dying man's breath. Yet, later, one after the other, it collects the corpses of the mutilated sounds and, like an ecstatic toddler only now learning to run, it awaits, awaits to be squandered again, Mr. Wagner it's heartbreaking, don't you think, I can't decide, had I been a fish in your head where I'd prefer to swim, in the Rhine's bed with the musical bubbles, or the bottom of the canals in Venice, in this silence never to be broken.*

Wagner wiped the sweat off his brow once again and finished his whiskey quietly. For the rest of the evening he did not turn his eyes to me. And I dared not address him anymore. I was thinking of the water in the canals of Venice, not a trace of air, thick, wrinkling irrevocably.

January Night at Mount Athos

What do I care about the purring of one who cannot love, like a cat?

- Friedrich Nietzsche

They were all wearing cat costumes. A kind of fur onesie in various colours. The tails probably had wire support because they always stood high. They all reached the glade at more or less the same time. It was pitch-dark; the moon was not up yet. As they passed in front of me, hidden as I was behind the bushes, they gave out a smell of red wine, incense, and fish roe. This was all taking place at a sort of open field, quite close to the convent, presumably where they disposed of the garbage. A dump so to speak. There was a number of bins around the field, all peculiarly shiny, resembling polished silverware, and full because the garbage overflowed.

The masqueraded monks kept silent. Only, every now and then, someone would be heard meowing, though not very convincingly. It appears as if this was their greeting. They all walked towards the seats positioned in a circle around an empty space in the field that they had obviously left as a stage where something was about to happen. They tread very softly; this makes the crickets cough. Nothing serious, though, just a light, abrupt little cough in the course of their smooth drone. Once all the seats were occupied, two monks dressed as cats emerged from one of the polished bins, each holding a bunch of small sacks. As they stepped into the centre of the makeshift stage, a sound resembling an imitation of that unfortunate purr erupted from the other monk's mouths. The January moon rose behind the mountain. Icy-blue, mouthless, a body of silence and nocturnal ice, a secret round hand-mirror that appears only when the prying eyes have turned elsewhere, or else it slashes them in half so that they don't see it.

The purring grew louder as the two monks opened the sacks and, on their imaginary stage, they freed several male cats of different sizes, ages, and colours. Then, they joined the rest of the seated monks and for a little while they all observed the panicked strides of the felines. From the opposite corner, another monk freed a female cat[9] among the males; the fake purring intensified. Suddenly I sensed someone's presence near me. I could not distinguish anyone in particular, only a shadow that could belong to a human, and the sound of breathing. I knew that if someone caught me there I would be

---

[9] Mount Athos is a peninsula full of monasteries at the North of Greece, inhabited exclusively by monks and hermits. Since Byzantine times, women are not permitted to enter this area, nor are any female animals with the sole exception of female cats.

in trouble as the only females allowed in the area are the cats.

Who's there? I whispered.

Shh, keep it down for the moon's sake, please.

It was Nietzsche, who crawled closer to me, between the branches and sat next to me. *You won't tell on me, will you?* His eyes sparkled in the night. *Look at them staring. It is their only chance at sinless courting.*

Nietzsche extended a paper bag of dried figs and offered me one. His manner of eating was similar to a magic trick; the figs kept disappearing in a mysterious black hole under his bushy moustache. Still munching, he went on talking.

Deep down, all they really wish is to jump out of a window. Yet, as you already know, the convent's windows are fitted with bars. Even if they were cats, as they so desire, they would still be house cats, not strays. Wasted souls, impotent vultures with a flaccid hunger. All their questions they satisfy with a purr. So little they ask from life that, the less it gives them, the more content their purring.

And the moon?

Hang on, you'll see.

A few minutes later, the moon was almost mid-sky. The cats' oi-oi, paired with the monks' purring, was almost deafening. The cats— just like their spectators—were now experiencing ecstasy in this public orgy. And then the moon shone on one of the polished bins and the garbage glowed, and kept glowing more and more, until we were almost blinded, I feared that my eyes would be slashed in half. Nietzsche's eyes, though, remained focused on the garbage light and under his moustache, still munching, I heard him murmur something, as if repeating a short prayer.

Salva me ab ore leonis, ne cadam in obscurum[10].

Well, I didn't know you were religious.

Let me remind you that the fig is my favourite fruit. Look!

I turned my eyes to where Nietzsche was looking and I saw myself and Nietzsche or two others who resembled us, reflected on the strange mirror of moonlight that illuminated the garbage. We were standing inside a beautiful garden. All around us tigers, lions, and panthers were licking their fur, purring and rubbing our feet. My hair was long as a veil. Nietzsche touches my fig leaf with his fingertips. With his free hand, he brings a fig to his mouth and it disappears magically under his bushy moustache. His mouth is like the bottom of a magician's hat. Our lips are moving, yet we don't make a sound.

---

[10] "Save me from the mouths of the lions, don't let me fall in darkness"; excerpt from the Latin funeral mass.

37

The Baker's Daughter

The rooster kept crowing all night, its crow sounding like the opening credits of "The Saint" with Roger Moore. Perhaps that's why everything in the deserted funfair was the washed out colour of the 60's. The children played with muddy water from the puddles. They let little white paper boats float and watched them soak in mud, turn brown and become completely absorbed by the surrounding misery, no trace of whiteness left behind them, no hope of quenching the thirst of memory. However, all the children looked like oversized angels painted by Raphael.

The rooster's crow functioned as a baroque alarm clock, only half-waking you up, its only use being the designation of sharp points within dreams, upon which you may touch your fingertip should you wish to wake up. One of the children approached me timidly. His friends were surrounding him, poking him, prompting him to talk to me about something that turned his cheeks red. Raphael, who had been discreetly supervising them all along, hidden behind a wall of ivy, showed himself in order to help the little boy and came up to me with a slightly expressionless look on his face.

The little guy is in love with you, he whispered in my ear, his voice grinning.

With me? How come?

He took you for a baker's daughter[11], *he likes bakers' daughters. He wants to kiss you.*

Then he returned to his post behind the wall of ivy and I could feel him peep. The boy came closer and touched his little palm upon my breast. I leaned down a little and let him touch his lips on mine. He didn't know how to kiss, he just drooled on my lips softly, while I stared absentmindedly on the electric sunbeams glowing inside his fair curls, and I saw something like a sunset covering that realm of mud with an unhoped-for kind of gold.

His saliva tasted like bâton salé. One of his buddies, an even younger one, pulled his sleeve to distract him. They both ran to the rickety seesaw, not bothering to glance at me. Raphael followed them tactfully and as he passed right next to me, as a reward, with his one hand he touched my breast, while with the other he put something in my palm secretly.

---

[11] Margherita Luti, also known as "La Fornarina", was the most famous of the many lovers of painter Raphael, a baker's daughter. There are two celebrated portraits of hers, in one of which she is dressed and in the other one nude. It is speculated that the fever that resulted in Raphael's death was brought on by an excessively passionate night he had spent with her.

As I walked away, I glanced behind me, on the inexplicably incomplete landscape. The rooster kept doing his Simon Templar crow, now making the children look monstrously similar to Roger Moore, whom I always compared to a sleazy cold fish, a combination of characteristics that could only apply to him. I squinted like a short-sighted person, unable to decide whether distance does not allow us to see things as they really are—since everyone is only able to see what is already inside their own eyes—or everything is actually a matter of perspective, which makes distance necessary in order to see things in their true dimensions.

I opened my palm to see what Raphael had given me and found a rose petal and a bâton salé, wrapped in a handwritten note.

If you were a baker's daughter, I would wrap you in a veil to strip you, I would sprinkle you with sugar to taste your savouriness, I would wait for you to become a rosebush and then I'd chop you to pieces, I would polish you, I would varnish you, I would turn you into my own bed on a high, brisk mountain-peak.

I took a bite of the bâton salé and it tasted like the Entombment. Suddenly, the obsessive crow of the rooster was the only familiar ingredient in the whole picture. It seemed as if it extended to infinity on both sides, a straight line upon which one may find all the time it takes to learn how to kiss and be kissed in precise equity. I wondered how Raphael kissed.

The theory of Beatrice Portinari[12]

on the other side

But already my desire and my will
were being turned like a wheel, all at one speed,
by the Love which moves the sun and the other stars

- Dante, *Paradiso*

Virgil Ivan "Gus" Grissom[13] is drinking lemonade on the moon. Every sip he takes is followed by a funny grimace of disgust; he's out of sugar and the lemonade is too sour. The lemonade is grey because everything on the moon is grey like a 50s TV screen, and so is the lemon tree that grows in Gus's garden. Gus is sitting in a chaise longue staring at planet Earth, which tonight is half-moon shaped. Everything on the moon is black and white but the Earth is in colour and Gus is peering at its vibrant portrait, constantly changing from an enigmatic profile to an elegant three-quarter view, then straight into a

---

[12] Beatrice Portinari (1266-1290) was the eternal platonic lover of the poet Dante. He fell in love with her when she was still 8 years old. She got married to a banker and died prematurely when she was 24. In the Divine Comedy, she is one of Dante's two guides in his journey through hell, purgatory and heaven.

[13] Lieutenant Colonel Virgil Ivan "Gus" Grissom (April 3, 1926 – January 27, 1967) was an iconic NASA astronaut who was killed in a pre-launch test of Apollo 1.

ruthless full face and vice versa. The pompous music of the celestial spheres is getting on his nerves; that's why he always listens to Patsy Cline on his walkman. *Sweet dreams of you* and so on. Tonight, Laika[14] is lying next to him, her ears drooping, and Gus is absentmindedly touching her snout now and then. Laika doesn't seem keen on playing; she's also just gazing at the earth absentmindedly.

Everything around them is moving ceaselessly, hence giving both of them the common illusion that they are the single motionless point in the universe. *I should hate you*, Patsy Cline keeps singing while Gus catches a glimpse of a red-haired lady in white, floating towards him among the stars. Everything about her is white apart from her green eyes and her long red hair, entangled in stardust as her face keeps changing constantly from an enigmatic profile into an elegant three-quarter view, then straight into a ruthless full portrait. Laika stands up and wags her tail.

You're late, says Gus, as the redhead kisses him lightly on the lips. *I thought I'd never see you again.*

The Almighty was feeling blue tonight. I brought some sugar for your lemonade, she replies, looking through a plastic supermarket bag covered in paintings of baby angels and then

---

[14] Laika (c. 1954 – 3 November 1957) was a stray dog from the streets of Moscow, the first animal to orbit the Earth in the Soviet spacecraft Sputnik 2 that was launched into outer space on 3 November 1957. Laika died within hours from overheating.

dropping it on the ground.

I was bored here, all by myself.

Well, you're not alone, you've got Laika. After all, it's the same story every night. If I'm a little late, you instantly assume I'm never coming back.

I'm jealous. I don't want you to go to him again. I don't want you to work there.

My sweet Gus, that's not possible and you know it.

I want you only for myself.

That's not possible either. This isn't just a job, it's the reason I exist. If I quit working at the supermarket, I will also quit existing. After all, I'm sure you do realise how important it is, what I do. It is a vast honour and responsibility offered to me by the Almighty.

I don't give a shit about the Almighty. I want you to move here so we can live together like a normal couple, me, you, the dog, our house, our lemon-tree...

Oh Gus, you know this cannot be...

I don't want you to go to this guy's freaking supermarket just to cheer up all the depressive tenants of Heaven, whom he bored to death while they were still alive only to keep boring them to eternity, I don't want you to do heaven knows what in his office. He's taking advantage of you, don't you understand?

It's you who doesn't understand, Gus.

I love you.

The only reason you love me is because you can't have me. And that's not your fault. That's my job. To make people fall in love with me. To inspire desire. It's a very important job. If I quit doing it, I will quit existing. And everything else around us will cease to exist. Because as long as they're in love with me, as long as I inspire desire, the sun and all the other stars will keep moving.

I don't give a shit about the sun and the stars and everyone. This is no movement, it's just meaningless compulsion, night and day, round and round, never arriving anywhere, there is no point. Is that all there is to it? I don't believe it, I just can't accept it.

When Patsy Cline opens her mouth, a white sheet of sobs tied in knots unfolds and you think that if you step on them you may climb all the way to the other side and, as long as Patsy Cline keeps her mouth open, you are thinking of the other side and all the customers of Heaven Supermarket are thinking of yet another other side which might even be right here.

The redhead is sitting on Gus's lap and folds her arms around his neck. Out of nowhere, a smile appears on his lips. He's happily rolling about on the green of her eyes, his childish laughter echoes across the universe. Next to him, Laika is barking, excited like a puppy. Patsy Cline's voice is the birds of Paradise mating. Everything is soaked in light and colours, everything is suspended within the youngest moment

46

time ever gave birth to, motionless in the midst of a world that keeps moving mechanically, transparent, neither before nor after, no dimensions, as light as an eyelash falling slowly.

That's all there is to it, my love.

The Baroque Toilet

To the splinter in T.W. Adorno's eye

All of a sudden I felt a pressing urge to pee. Since running I find unnatural (and so I never run), I rushed calmly toward the corridor with the wooden doors, facing one another in two endless rows. I pushed a random door open, to find myself in a cubicle with dazzlingly white tiling. Through the glass roof, the autumn sun drooled golden rays all around me, covering everything with a brightness as thick as custard cream and jelly, while a beam of light fell on the toilet bowl in the middle of the booth. Now, toilets I always found grim, objects to invite rampant loneliness, empty moments in the company of one's most basic self, until then inexplicably and magnificently ignored. It is perhaps because of this aversion that I tame my own natural needs and achieve a mere two visits daily to this temple of wasted productivity. Imagine, then, if you will, my surprise with this insufferable urge to pee that afternoon.

As I opened the door, he turned abruptly and faced

me. And I, in my turn, returned his inquisitive stare as it tickled its way around my body, a rather unwelcome sensation at that time of limited self-control. Apparently, Adorno had been inspecting the toilet bowl meticulously as I walked in, an object I now noticed to be indeed worthy of detailed study. A thick layer of golden acanthus leaves sprawled from the toilet cistern to its lid, made of marble itself and decorated with round rubies, and there wasn't a spot on the seat not covered with emeralds, gold leaf, engravings of human faces and wild beasts, with this inexplicably baroque decoration extending even above the toilet cistern, as if this queer nexus had a life of its own, breathing and expanding, engulfed within its own tender friction, until the moment I opened the door and forced it into stifled immobility, a shift that also prompted Adorno's abrupt reaction.

He was wearing a burgundy silk robe with a Japanese pattern, and matching slippers.

Oh, what pointy ears you have!

All the better to rest my round glasses.

And, oh, what round glasses you have!

All the better for keeping splinters in my eyes.

He turned once again to the toilet seat and, as I moved closer, I noticed that he was only pretending to be examining the sculpture, his eyes rather fixed on something inside the bowl. I moved closer, so close that my head touched his own hairless head, but Adorno did not appear to mind it. I was looking for a way to tell him to leave already so that I could finally pee, but I felt shy. We stood above the bowl, our heads touching for a long time, with Adorno's eyes fixed upon the water with anguish. It was only then that I noticed something floating down there, as I heard him ask me:

What do you reckon it is? What do you see!

A frankfurter.

A frankfurter? But it's so red!

He groped his groin nervously, looked back at me with anger and shame, and then Adorno tightened his robe's belt melodramatically and left the booth visibly shaken.

You savage! I murmured, and flushed the toilet.

The mysterious red frankfurter disappeared down the drain. Mixed with the sound of the running water, Adorno's muffled sobbing echoed in the corridor.

An Anniversary

For our anniversary you gave me an electric nosferatu. During the day he recharges and at night he sneaks into bed next to me. All night I dream of a freshly chopped piano with milk teeth. Sometimes I touch it with the tips of my nails and the teeth tremble a little and start pushing each other, the piano becomes a gigantic black-and-white rattle, spitting out clanging names incapable of inhabiting a human mouth. This dream resembles a pendulum, its shape swinging between a miniscule moment of immobility and a dispersal longing for silence.

Meanwhile, the electric nosferatu drinks all my blood and in the darkness the only sounds are his gulps sliding gently down his Adam's apple, and something he whispers in my ear incessantly, breathlessly, as if inhaling in whispers, and all night he tells me of crinkly fig leaves and of lovers shedding skin. He tells me of the place where forgotten dreams go, of the pebbles I dropped behind me for you to find me and they are now rattling in his own pocket, but most of all he likes talking about blood, my blood, flowing warm in his throat, my blood becoming his blood every night, about the gentle embrace of the shadows, sweeter than those of bodies, and about my own body that he is emptying tenderly in this reverse intercourse. By the break of dawn he's told me everything, each night the same exhalation-poem.

Then I get out of bed to take my breakfast in the kitchen. The kitchen is at the end of the corridor with the 88 doors. Usually, before I make it to the end of the corridor, exactly mid-way to be precise, I stage a collapse and lie on the floor, striking an adorably melancholy pose, eyes shut, focusing my attention on hearing your approaching footsteps echoing on the marble floor in the empty house. After I establish that there is not a single sound, for even the clocks hold their breath and their hands are still, at last I proceed to the kitchen. I sit by the table and stare absentmindedly at the cage with the little deaf-mute nightingale, opening and closing its beak noiselessly. It is like a love-call, what it does. Most probably it's unaware that its song is mute. For hours, I can sit there and watch the bird's conviction that the partner it thinks it's calling will fly through the open window any minute now.

It all takes some getting used to, it all takes some getting used to, I tell the bird, don't worry, the good and the bad, it all takes some getting used to, the good and the bad, that's why you ought to, everything takes some getting used to, that's why you ought to worry. Everything, the blooming cadenzas and the walks along the pier, the crumpled sheets and the broken glances, the crimps on one's hair, the uncomfortable silences, the words still soft like unformed embryos, everything takes some getting used to whether you like it or not you'll get used to everything, you will get used to liking everything, as much as you would've gotten used to disliking everything; whether you worry or not. You will get used to worrying; you will get used to not worrying. And then you will get used to having gotten used to.

It is not you who's standing behind me. It is someone whose face I recognise without seeing. He is standing behind me, going through my pockets, touching my cheeks. It is not you. To comfort me he recites words with soft t's. And under his fingertips all is as white as an ending.

Jack and the Potato-stalk
or The Lernaean Dietrich

Jack lived in Exarchia, Athens. In a tiny studio on the mezzanine of an old block of flats. He had a tiny balcony facing the lightwell, so he had to stick his head out of the balcony door first thing every morning in order to check the weather, and he had to look high, as high as he could to catch a glimpse of the colour of the sky. It was there Jack planted a potato plant. He planted it in a pot on the tiny balcony and watered it every day.

One night, Jack dreamt that Marlene Dietrich had fallen in love with him. He was trying to slip away from her but she would always discover him, no matter where he would hide. In the last frame of his dream, Jack had shut himself in an ice cream freezer, with the help of the ice cream man. *She'll never find you in here*, said the ice cream man. *Oh, and don't even think of trying the ice cream, it's really old*, he added and shut the glass freezer door on top of Jack. A couple of minutes later, he heard a husky breeze approaching and the stale ice cream started melting with admiration. He instantly saw Marlene Dietrich's head appear amongst the fluorescent wrappers.

Jack woke up dripping with sweat. He went out on the tiny balcony to have a smoke. Just for an instant, he thought he caught a glimpse of Marlene Dietrich's trench coat in the corner of the balcony and then a tiny part of her gleaming negligee a bit further away. He shook his head really hard to awaken himself a bit more and lit a cigarette. The moment he began to relax, he took a look at his potato plant, cigarette hanging from his lips like a numb limb. The potato plant had grown so much in just a few hours, that the thick green stalk had broken out of the iron railing on the balcony, already stretching all over the lightwell. He gaped at the plant in amazement as it kept growing rapidly, while he could hear its shoots and leaves stretch higher and higher in the dead of night, a soft humming reminiscent of cogwheels of steel and velvet slowly rubbing against each other.

Jack had no idea what to do. He didn't even dare to imagine the janitress' reaction when she would discover the entire lightwell covered in potato leaves the following morning. Also, according to his elementary gardening knowledge, potatoes are ripe as soon as the leaves wither and fall off the plant; this is when you dig up the potatoes.

This particular potato plant, however, wasn't showing any intention to wither. No sir, far from it. That's when he decided to uproot the plant. He decided that he would hurry outside, to the garbage bin down the road and he would shove it in there as best he could. He had to act fast because the potato plant kept growing manically and in a little while he wouldn't have any control over the situation. He rolled up his pyjama sleeves and started pulling the roots with all his might, his foot pushing against the balcony railing.

Jack lives in Exarchia, Athens. He had a potato plant he uprooted. When he tried to dig up the potatoes, he found seven tiny Marlene Dietrichs, wearing negligees under their trenchcoats. Now every morning, they prepare seven Greek coffees for him and they stick their seven perfect tiny heads out of the balcony door in order to tell him what the weather is like. Every afternoon he takes them out for a walk down Benaki street and they steal seven stale ice creams from the ice cream man for Jack's sake. They sleep with him every night, on his tiny sofa-bed. Before they lie down next to him, they take their seven trench coats off, all of them at once, and Jack gets seven goosebumps.

Passacaglia[15]

Lully could be whatever he wished. For example, he is crazy about ice creams. Therefore, he could be an ice cream man; only he looks pale in white. He could have chosen any sedentary profession, the civil service for instance, or become a secretary, an accountant, a cashier at a supermarket or a ticket booth, he could be a truck driver, a cabbie, and a pianist. He could even take the piss out of his disability and utilize his amputated leg to start a career at a sector where such an attribute is an asset, a pirate for example, or a super hero with a special power that renders it irrelevant, like flying or invisibility or kicking things all the way to the moon. Lully gives this variety of professional choice due attention and then dismisses each option for different reasons. He has never been into Math, he is hypochondriac with banknotes and always washes his hands after touching one, cars have not been invented yet, neither have trains, nor the piano, his handwriting is unbearable, he despises rum, he is scared of heights, and he would never risk disfiguring his beloved moon's façade.

---

[15] The Passacaglia is a musical form of the Baroque era, originating from a Spanish 17th century dance. Its main characteristic is a repeating bass in a three beat rhythm.

It is almost mid-day and Lully is taking a walk in the gardens of the Versailles. Standing in the middle of a glade, he stares at his shadow shifting in size and shape, as the sun strolls the sky. His leg is somewhat itching, but his shadow can't feel anything, he thinks, neither can the light-hearted spring breeze, nor the pain in his gangrened foot, in need of immediate amputation. Lully's shadow could truly become whatever it wished. Lully's shadow appears indestructible. It is perhaps its ability to reinvent itself that makes it so. Lully stays still, waiting for the sun to come straight above his head, observing his shadow moving closer and reaching an imaginary vertical stand. Lully becomes one with his shadow, trying to feel that he himself could be whatever he wished. Eyes shut, he is striving to imagine a different self, it's all in your head Mssr Lully, no need to become trapped in your own self-image, we are versatile creatures, as long as we don't obsess over our obsessions that is, Mssr Lully, snap out of yourself, you could be whatever in the world you wished, just choose something, life is great and definitely more important than our choices, feel the carelessness of the spring breeze, the sun warm on your cheeks in the middle of the Versailles gardens, Mssr Lully, come to your senses, live, become someone else, and live.

Lully is heading back to his private apartments. On the way, he takes a few moments in front of his marble statue, somewhere among the flowerbeds. He admires his marble calves, his long fingers holding the conducting staff, and he can imagine his naked feet inside the pointy shoes, tracing the steps of a passacaglia on the ground. Is it that most people have this privilege of becoming what they wish, he wonders, or is it rather that the majority wish to become what they can. He also wonders if it is even easier to become what one wishes when one's wishes are not exact, and whether what one wishes obstructs what they could become, and in the end whether it is better to want or to wish. He turns back and watches his shadow follow him at a steady ¾ pace. Yes, Lully[16] could have become whatever he wished. And all he wants to do is dance.

---

[16] Jean-Baptiste Lully (1632-1687) was a French composer in the court of Louis the XIV. While conducting in a concert, he accidentally stabbed his leg with his conductor's baton. When the doctors suggested that his leg should be amputated, he refused as he would not bear to live without being able to dance. As a result, he died of gangrene that spread in his entire body and brain.

Agnus Dei

Dolly is staring at the grass. It's just grass as far as her eye can see. No trees or anything else. Just grass under the blue sky and the white clouds. Dolly is squinting, trying to focus on a single blade of grass but she doesn't seem to manage. The moment she thinks her eye has caught a specific blade, all of a sudden she isn't certain anymore whether it still is that initial blade she had her eyes set on and then she goggles at the grass, once again allowing it to become an enormous blot of green in the midst of which she is standing.

Dolly is staring at the clouds. The clouds are travelling above her head, softly pushed by the light breeze. Dolly is concentrating on one cloud at a time, trying to figure out what it looks like. But the moment she names it, the breeze has already transformed it into something entirely different she hadn't even imagined until then. It only takes a few milliseconds for a gentleman who is about to take a sip from a cracked teacup to turn into an unripe star falling off the wrinkled universe.

Dolly is staring at the sky. She is staring insistently, manically and then shuts her eyes abruptly only or a moment, trying to hold that blue inside her eyes, beneath her eyelids. Dolly is wondering if anyone else knows this trick and feels excited with the idea that she is the only creature who knows how to hold an entire blue sky under her eyelids for a moment.

Dolly's mother gave birth to her following an immaculate conception. Her father was a strange guy with a bushy beard. Her godfather picked this name for her because he was a huge fan of Dolly Parton. Dolly has the same dream every single night. She's in a stable with no roof, seated on a golden throne and she has seven eyes and seven horns. There are crowds of people all around her, pushing and cursing in tongues she doesn't quite understand, tears are flowing from their eyes, each one of them is holding a sword in one hand and a perfectly round cup in the other, while the crowd is spread out as far as her eye can see and beyond.

Dolly is squinting, trying to focus on one single person but she doesn't seem to manage. The moment she thinks her eye has caught a specific person, all of a sudden she isn't certain anymore whether it still is that initial person she had her eyes set on and then she goggles at the crowd, once again allowing it to become an enormous blot of flesh in the midst of which she is standing.

Then one of them escapes from the crowd and manages to approach her. Dolly isn't sure whether he will use his sword to slaughter her or his cup to water her. But the moment she decides, the crowd has already pulled him back, turning him again into a fraction of the amorphous mass of bodies surrounding her.

Dolly shuts all seven eyelids and feels seven hands grabbing her seven horns. She feels swords piercing her body. She holds her seven eyelids tightly shut and all she can see is the blue sky, not just for one moment, now her eyes have multiplied and so are the moments. As soon as Dolly feels seven times as excited with her uniqueness, she hears her blood flowing in the perfectly round cups and its smell awakens her.

The grass is always greener on the other side of the fence, her father used to tell her with British phlegm. Yet Dolly can't see a fence anywhere. She finds this quite disappointing; fences can prove immensely useful in such occasions, now where is she supposed to look for the greener grass, where is she supposed to find that place where everyone who is different from the rest goes to find each other and pretend they are more like each other than the rest, only to realise that they are not so alike either and to start looking for the next fence? She can't see any other creature like her anywhere either. Just like every single blade of grass, despite the spiteful nonsense that is commonly believed about her species, she feels different from all the rest, all those who differ from each other in the same old ways. *Yes, that's it, that's it*, ponders Dolly, *it is the way you differ that counts, not merely the fact that you differ, that's a given*, and then decides to give in to her lowly craving, modestly chomping on the grass trying to ignore the same old protests of every single blade of grass, yelling at her *hey, you can't eat me, I am not like all the others*, he pretends she cannot hear, but how could she after all, Dolly is just a sheep, perhaps not exactly like all the others, but she's still a sheep

73

getting hungry, grazing, bleating ba ba ba even though for a moment I thought that I could hear her thoughts with my extraordinary ears, it wasn't thoughts, it was yet another ba of yet another unsuspecting creature, grazing, bearing the sins of the world, the same old different same old way, blabbering on and on ba ba ba.

Just add water

I dreamt that I had dreamt of what I would be dreaming.
When I opened my eyes, Lewis Carroll was asleep next to me, on the
green fainting couch. A set of china was set on the tea table. The tea was
getting cold in the teapot. The teacups had obviously been used, lipstick
stains highlighting the tiny cracks on the brims. With my fingertip, I
picked up one lemon cake crumb from each saucer. The pink roses
decorating the porcelain were still buds when I opened my eyes, on the
green fainting couch, right next to Lewis Carroll. My eyes are stinging;
two tear marshes had been sprouting on my eyeballs. Lemon cake on
the tongue, salt in the eyes; remnants are always a certainty, even when
it comes to tearful tea parties.

Sometimes, when I'm awake, images of myself getting ready
to do various strange things appear in my head. They seem like photos

75

taken from a stranger's retro photo-album, bought in some vintage shop clearance. I, biting the brim of a very thin glass; I, dragging my belly on a long and sharp piece of darkness; I, struggling to walk through the green corridor; I, laying motionless on the sidewalk; I, preparing to put on a white coat in the midst of a swamp; I, picking lemon cake crumbs with my fingertip; I, rubbing my eyes, the dried up tear marshes stinging; I, scraping off the salt meticulously, collecting it in my palm, sprinkling it in a pot of boiling water; I, uncovering the teapot, finding a tuft of baby hair at the bottom; I, preparing hot beverages with the remains, boiling the salt from my dried up tears, drinking, weeping, collecting the tear salt yet again and everything must begin once more, repeating in a loop of nostalgic paralysis.

Lewis Carroll will open his eyes and will have two tiny parasols instead of eyebrows. That's why his eyes are always moist and sleepy. The sun never touches them and when Lewis Carroll looks at something dry, it moistens and the world around him seems to be floating within a wet dream. He will have the gaze of a tired baby, born through the mouth of a ravenous monster, a baby that had to use his tender hands to open a jaw of sharp teeth in order to get out into this world, wrapped in the saliva of the famished beast, and then dropped on a fluffy blanket. Not a scratch. No trace of monster on his skin. Perhaps it was the thump of the falling baby that woke me up, but then again, who knows how long I have been waking up for. This is no laughing matter, it may take years.

Lewis Carroll will be looking at me while I'll be waking up, the way he was looking at me while I was dreaming that I had dreamt of what I would be dreaming. He will want me to take him with me in my dream, where we are sleeping next to each other on the fainting couch, amongst the memorabilia of a tearful tea party. And I know this is not possible. But he insists on wanting it. That's why he will wear a top hat, he will turn the edges of his melancholy lips upwards, he will fix them there, and then he will cut the lemon cake and serve the beverage of tears and baby tufts. There will be soft music, pipes and flutes of sugarcane. And Lewis Carroll will start looking for something in his lapel pocket, something protruding like an obscene miniature. He will find a red lipstick, he will apply it on my lips, check if it's straight, and then he will put it back in his pocket, looking satisfied. Then he will peer at me, he will squeeze my lips with his fingertips until they turn into a tiny red heart and he will turn the edges of his lips downwards again until his mouth resembles a thread whose ends are hanging straight to the centre of the earth and I let my eyes follow them, I follow them lower and lower, my gaze falling fast, down, down, down, lower and deeper, a cracked thin glass, a bloodstained sharp piece of darkness, two footprints on a green corridor, a chalk outline on the sidewalk, a muddy white coat, withered porcelain rose-petals, lemon cake crumbs stuck on a fingertip, my finger on my mouth and the lipstick stains highlighting the tiny cracks on the brim of a teacup, remnants, traces, my traces, a green fainting couch, a Lewis Carroll and I, two figures posing opposite each other on a playing card in the hand of someone who dreamt that

77

he had dreamt that he would be dreaming of us.

La Dolce Vita and the multiplication of the stale loaves

It is common knowledge that Saints frequent Paradise; that place where the air smells of brand new plastic, unused, pastures are green and skies are cloudless—that is, apart from special occasions, such as when a somewhat melancholy angel doesn't feel like using his wings and therefore prefers to stay hidden in a fluffy cloud in order to avoid the fingers and looks that would get fixed on her should he choose to fly over the hills of paradise, since wings, even in paradise, are pointed at and, as we all know, fingers leave fingerprints.

The day of a Saint is very strictly structured, not because of a plethora of activities but due to their lack. In other words, their days are so strictly empty that the void keeps piling up on top of its identical everyday versions with chilling precision. Needless to say, nothing is forbidden in Paradise; after all, what sort of paradise would that be? However, the reason why nothing is forbidden is actually the fact that its residents have already forbidden themselves almost everything, even pastimes that seem absolutely innocent to the unsuspecting eye of a sinner, since only the suspiciously innocent eye of a Saint may perceive the perilous temptations lurking all around us.

So, Saints are up by the break of dawn every morning. This is unavoidable, since drapes or curtains of all sorts don't exist in this verdant resting place. This ensures unrestricted access of the eye of God to all places of paradise simultaneously. God detests curtains, but above all, he hates pulling them to see what it is they're hiding. After they awaken, they go for a walk, always alone. The Saints only look straight ahead, never turning their heads right or left, so the only way for them to meet is face to face, or "tête-à-tête" if you like, or to literally bump into each other at the point where two straight lines cross.

Saints have very delicate features and their limbs, especially their extremities, are unusually long and frail. That's why they avoid handshakes, as the lack of flesh causes an uncomfortably bony sensation and they prefer to greet each other through imaginary verbose gestures they carve in the air. However, the most distinctive part of the Saints' body is their mouth, always clenched in a disgusted snob expression. That's why, wherever you go in paradise, you see stiff upper lips facing each other, not a trace of a kiss in between them, stuck in suspended tedium.

This somewhat condescending expression is usually due to the Saints' inability to fill the eternity that is spread everywhere ahead of them, as far as their eye can see, horribly sun-drenched. Their only way to kill time is exchanging little pieces of their holy relics, sometimes throwing them on the heads of priests the moment they least expect it, as an occasional and not-so-gentle reminder of who has the upper hand.

Sometimes again, they spend hours sitting under all sorts of holy trees, praying, fasting, repenting, multiplying loaves, signing indulgentiae, spraying that 80's aftershave for men who don't have to try too hard on lilies or training pigeons to sit on the heads of heroic statues and that's how their days go by without any traces.

Yet, sometimes they secretly live it up a little. They wait for the night to come and just before the moon sets, they go down to the Fontana di Trevi. It is the only time when there's no one around, except for an unmarried couple or a drunkard sleeping it off on the steps. They would sell their souls to the devil for an ice cream but the gelateria is closed. They lift their mantles a little, dip their feet in the fountain and gaze at the skeleton-coloured non-light sky. They gaze at the tilted moon, flirting with them, posing as Anita Ekberg. A few feet away, five or six baby angels are playing with their watercolours. With their baby hands, they cover each other's skin with paintings of oversized private parts and burst into laughter. The Saints wait patiently for their toes to get pruney. They collect some pennies from the bottom of the fountain and stuff them in their pockets. They just can't wait to fall asleep with the wasted wishes of mortals under their pillows.

Coprolalia

Oui, by the love of my skin,
I shit on your nose, so it runs down your chin.

- Wolfgang Amadeus Mozart, letter to his cousin

He could hardly restrain his excitement that morning. While waiting for the waitress to bring him his coffee, he kept repeating last night's conversation with the doctor again and again in his head, a discussion that had shown him the path to a new life. He kept repeating it again and again, trying to soothe a somewhat intolerable euphoric feeling he was taken over with since the operation had finished successfully and he had walked through the threshold of the clinic, as light as ever, a new man.

Please describe in as much detail as possible the manner in which your thoughts become unbearable.

My thoughts are unbearable to me in three different ways. First of all, there are the thoughts that cause me inexplicable distress. They always appear out of the blue, usually at times when I feel totally relaxed. For example, I'm lying on the couch with a girl I really fancy and we are making out. As soon as I start feeling quite content, a thought occurs—a thought I am unable to stop—that the lady uproots my testicles, lifts them up in the air and starts screaming in the living room like Conan the Barbarian. Or, as I walk down the street on a fine spring morning, I listen to the birds chirping happily and the very next second I think of the birds attacking me and devouring my eyes. Of course, I sought psychiatric help for this tormenting symptom. Yet, every single psychiatrist failed to spot any disturbance in the rest of my behaviour; they all assured me that it was kind of normal to occasionally have such macabre or violent thoughts, that they are no cause for alarm as long as I don't confuse them with reality and therefore this slight disturbance does not prevent me from leading an otherwise perfectly normal life. There are also the thoughts that infuriate me. You would be right to say that this is not very original either. But listen, here's what the trouble is; while I am not quick-tempered, on the contrary, I am very polite, I watch my mouth, I don't become aggressive even if someone, say, harms me or becomes rude or unfair to me, but there are moments when, again out of the blue, I have these thoughts that wouldn't normally enrage me, yet suddenly make me absolutely furious for no obvious reason. For instance, I may be in a modern art gallery—you know, I often go to such places just to hang out, otherwise modern art leaves me indifferent—and while I'm indifferently looking at yet another installation with bricks and broken corkscrews, a tribute to incessant immobility and the futility of transformation, it suddenly occurs to me that I am so furious with this bland place and that I want to smash everything in there, even though I have no clue why. But the third and worst type of thought that torments me and has actually forced me to seek your help is all the rest of my thoughts. They are so dull they make me loathe myself; thoughts that are excruciatingly banal, cliché, uninspired, thoughts of disgusting mediocrity. Not too dumb, yet not too smart. Just this horrific "nothing special". The everyday thoughts of the ordinary man. What time should I leave to catch the bus, is there any rice left, who keeps leaving brochures in my letterbox, should I get an anatomic pillow, are the ads too long in this show, how fattening is fried chicken, are purple or yellow flowers best for the living room tapestry, and so on.

Alright, alright, I get it.

So? Is there any hope? I understand that what I'm going through is nothing original. I guess that most people have the same issue. But I can't take it anymore, I want to put an end to this, I am very unhappy.

I think I might be able to help you out. Let's do a recap. As far as I understand, your thoughts are basically dull and sometimes upset you, that is, they terrify you, if you allow me, or infuriate you.

Precisely.

Well, I think I have a solution. Thought transplant is a relatively new operation but I believe it is worth trying. It is absolutely painless, it only takes a few minutes and you may choose the thoughts of any person you like, as long as their thoughts are on our database of course.

It sounds spectacular. But how to choose, doctor? This is tremendously hard.

Perhaps I already have something in mind. Tell me, please, what sort of music do you listen to? Do you enjoy Mozart?

Mozart? I am crazy about Mozart!

Aha! I thought so. How would you feel about a transplant of Mozart's thoughts into your own brain? Sharp, a genius with a sense of humour as well as depth in his thought. Don't you think it's a superb idea?

It certainly was a superb idea. The transplant had lasted just 19 manures, er sorry, minutes, and the doctor was extremely satisfied with the procedure. While he waited for his coffee, sitting at the bamboo table that morning when the sun was shining after a shitormy, er sorry, stormy night, and everything was glistening around him as if everything obscure or old had been washed off, or as if god had a weak bladder and was pissing his holy piss all night long on the heads of his unsuspecting creatures, he could already feel his new, borrowed thoughts forming inside his skull, spreading all over his neurons with a kind of euphoria, whose gentle simplicity was comparable only to a morning defecation after a cup of coffee. The waitress arrived with his coffee just in time, while he happily enjoyed the unique sensation that he might still be a common man yet in his brain he now carried the thoughts of a genius. *No more banalities; angelic melodies and sophisticated thoughts will be echoing in my head from now on,* he thought and pinched the waitress's bottom. The waitress let out a little scream of astonishment and struck him on the head with her tray. *Shit,* he thought. *Shit, shit, shit, shit*[17], he thought again, and the letters of this word, which had probably never crossed his mind before, started getting in line, climbing on imaginary staves dripping with shit too, forming obscene nursery rhymes with a giggle. Wherever

---

[17] Mozart was well known for his scatological sense of humour, which is very clearly illustrated in his correspondence. In the beginning of the 20th century, psychologists did some research that led some of them to believe that this might prove the composer suffered from Tourette's syndrome.

he looked, the world seemed like an endless playground full of shit, where everyone rolled about joyfully, grabbing each other's ass, farting loudly and making funny faces.

He was in shock and kept staring at his coffee in the cup, now looking and smelling like steaming shit, an image that made him laugh uncontrollably, the laughter of creatures swallowing shit and shitting music.

The transplant was a success.

Impromptu with statue

To Margot Wölk (1917-2014),
one of Adolf Hitler's food tasters

A cringing dull reality show is constantly being played behind Adolf Hitler's eyelids. Eyes-wide-open-Adolf is standing on top of an obelisk, on his tiptoes, barefoot, in his pyjamas, his eyes painfully getting dry, struggling not to shut his eyes. Eyes-quite-shut-Adolf is watching the cringing dull reality show, casually lying on the couch, in the dusk, on his cute beer-belly lays a pack of peculiar snacks he's chewing tediously, the pack softly moving up and down along with his cute beer-belly and the snacks crumble on Adolf's fingers as he brings them to his mouth. The ends of Adolf's eyes are grinning, oh how he'd love to rub this grin in his mom's face, *Adolf darling, don't look so grim, and don't forget your jacket*, she used to tell him every time he was getting ready for a kids' party. She would get on his nerves so much that for the entire party he would just sit on a chair, silent and stern, drawing colourful swastikas on the napkins with his crayons. He would watch all the cringing dull kids devour meatballs and cocktail sausages and he would get so mad at the thought of all the poor animals that had been slaughtered in order to fill the unbearably useless hours of a tedious childhood with their flesh.

91

He was disgusted by all those two-legged creatures who ravaged all the rest of the species as a trivial snack, convinced as they were of their own race's superiority. They disgusted him and made him dream of a utopian world of justice, where human beings would only be allowed to consume human meat. Such thoughts are going through his mind faintly, as he gnaws on the Jew-shaped vegetarian snacks that have been custom-made for him by his scientific team, while he cannot even imagine how many devout vegetarians will get into fights with fanatic meat-eaters in the future, precisely because of his strictly vegetarian diet, oh *my poor darling Adolf, don't listen to them, I know you meant well,* his mom would have said.

Meanwhile eyes-wide-open-Adolf is inhaling the fresh air on top of the obelisk, and pretends to be a statue. Pigeons sit on his head to get some rest. The moon's pointy edges tickle his nostrils. Parachutists wave at him and tease him but he doesn't bat an eyelid. *Well done darling Adolf, stay still for the school photo, otherwise you'll be blurry in all eternity.* The obelisk is high—so high it nearly touches the clouds—and passersby pause and look through their binoculars, trying to see who it is up there on top of such a high obelisk, but to be honest, nobody has binoculars, after all why carry binoculars when one takes a walk to the centre or the market or the bank, binoculars are no use, there are hardly any worthwhile wild animals left in the centre, they don't sell rare birds in the market anymore, just clockwork birds, and it's been a while since they've put up an impromptu opera show or an improvised coital session in a bank, that's why they don't really look through their binoculars, they just put their hands over their eyes pretending they are trying to see far, high, up there on the very top of the obelisk, nearly all the way to the clouds, they look but they don't see, they just stand there, beneath Adolf's shadow, telling each other, *he must have been a great man.*

The Revenge of Cloclo

In this city everything is perfect. People are loving and helpful to each other. They all have a job and they're all perfectly happy with their jobs. Lovers never lie to each other and never fall out of love. The weather is always just right for the season. There is no hunger, poverty, evil, illness, violence, misery. All is perfect in this city. All but one thing; wherever you go, streets, supermarkets, offices, restaurants, beaches, gyms, public toilets, elevators, even inside every single apartment, there are speakers playing songs by Claude Francois, aka Cloclo. By Claude Francois only. Non-stop, any time of day (and night). Nobody remembers how, when, or why this had been decided. It must have happened several generations back because it all seems perfectly natural to everyone; nobody seems to be paying the slightest attention to this constant musical accompaniment, underlining awkwardly their everyday routine as well as the most significant moments of their lives. Everyone is fine with it, apart from an organisation called Bouche Fermée. Bouche Fermée set off as a small collective, but have recently declared themselves rebels, consisting of around ten percent of the population, citizens who are not particularly fond of this specific musical background and are determined to do all they can to finally silence the speakers in the entire city.

Bouche Fermée have registered numerous official complaints, signed petitions, compiled manifestos, at some point they even organised demonstrations, but, naturally, all their marches, revolutionary mottos, and fiery speeches seemed terribly ridiculous under the sounds of Cloclo's songs, such as *Laisse-moi t'aimer, Alexandrie Alexandra*, or *Magnolias forever*. Passersby paused for a while, thinking it must be some kind of farce or a humorous art installation and burst into laughter, especially when the peak of the Bouche Fermée chief's speech would coincide with the somewhat melodramatic tune of *Comme d'habitude*.

All their petitions to pause Cloclo's music were rejected by the council, without even giving them a chance to discuss their plea with a high-rank officer. The official response was always the same. *We regret to inform you that your appeal has been rejected, as your organisation represents only a negligible portion of the population. The vast majority feels absolutely delighted with the musical accompaniment in our city, a city ruled by the principles of democracy. We are sorry you are unable to appreciate Cloclo's beneficial qualities and we hope to be able to satisfy one of your future requests, as long as it complies with the public sentiment.*

After failing to fight for their rights the legal way, the Chief decided it was time to take matters in their own hands, hoping that violence would finally lead somewhere. The first blow has been scheduled for tonight, midnight. Three members of the organisation have sneaked in the central government building, from which all the speakers in town are controlled. The Chief is waiting for them in a car outside the building. His face is rather ordinary, everything about him is ordinary, apart from his eyebrows, which bring to mind a capital L, in a 90 degree rotation, as if someone had pushed it by accident, or not, and the L had fallen on its face. *Si j'avais un marteau*, the speakers are playing softly, and he's giggling because it seems rather ironic to him that his men are about to smash the central sound system with a hammer, while this specific song is playing.

He's counting the seconds, waiting for the moment he's been waiting for since he was a kid, and to which he has dedicated his entire life. He's waiting to hear the silence. He remembers all those life moments destroyed because of this guy's miserable songs, and he utterly hates this guy, even though he knows absolutely nothing about him, because he can't even bear to hear his name, he never wanted to know anything about him, yet to him he is the most hateful person in the world, someone he has absolutely nothing in common with. It's been years he's been feeling he can't actually live seriously with this musical accompaniment, he feels he has wasted his youth trying to exist within this sonic monstrosity and cannot grasp the inexplicable acoustic immunity of 90 percent of the population, who manage to live absolutely normally under these circumstances. He's thinking of love confessions with *Reverie*, job interviews under the sound of *Belles belles belles*, funerals with *Le lundi au soleil*, insomniac nights with *Le jouet extraordinaire*, and all this absurdity infuriates him.

The three saboteurs are running very late and he's now beginning to get worried something has gone terribly wrong. He leaves the car and enters the government building, feeling prepared for everything. He finds a couple of guards lying unconscious in the corridor. Everything is very quiet, if the idea of quietness can possibly even be imagined within the sounds of Cloclo's disco hit, *Eve*. As he walks into the main control room, he finds his three men standing over a mixing deck. They are motionless, their eyes fixed on the main switch and the ominous sign above it: *Danger: Do Not Touch*. He approaches them and they stare at him, their eyes filled with tears.

We can't do it, Chief.

What does this mean? We are comrades fighting for a common cause. We must press the fucking switch if we really want our voice to be heard at last.

Perhaps it's not that bad the way it is.

You are cowards.

We've never actually heard how silence sounds like, how can you be so sure we're going to like it?

You are ridiculous.

You go ahead and do it, then. We just can't take this responsibility.

Without thinking twice, he touches his finger on the switch. It is the moment he's been waiting his entire life. He's already ecstatic at the thought that he is about to change the world with a single touch of his finger. Even the moment he's electrocuted[18], he's smiling. The last image to pass before his eyes is his capital L shaped eyebrows. When he was a little boy his mother used to tell him that many great leaders had strange eyebrows. And he's thinking, like he used to back then, that many beautiful words have their roots in L. Life, Love, Laughter, Light, Liberty. The capital L looks like a crooked hairpin left upon the blackness of a true love's hair, according to another song, sung countless times in some other nearby city.

---

[18] Claude Francois, singer of Comme d'habitude, the original French version of My Way, died in 1978, aged 39. While taking a shower, he tried to straighten a light-bulb and was electrocuted.

Confucius' fake news

I do not feel obliged to believe that the same God who has endowed us with sense, reason, and intellect has intended us to forgo their use.

- Galileo Galilei, 1615 letter to Duchess Christina of Tuscany

They say that Confucius had said: *When the wise man points at the moon, the idiot looks at the finger.* Galileo's middle finger is exhibited at the Museo Galileo in Florence. Some admirers of his stole the body while it was being moved to a new tomb and after a series of adventures, the finger ended up in the museum. Galileo's middle finger is still pointing at the sky. The prudish ones, or perhaps the ones who look at the moon rather than the finger, say that after all those centuries, it's still pointing at the sky and they find this very moving, a symbol of the triumph of the human spirit, an offering of hope to humanity.

I, on the other hand, in spite of risking being taken for an idiot, I only see a finger that's *pointed* in proud vulgarity towards the sky or, perhaps, towards another form of idiocy that many of us have realised or suspected has been occupying the space right above us; some inches above, a few floors, social classes or levels of power, or even a few imaginary celestial spheres. I see Galileo's finger courageously pointed in the face of oppressive fathers, bossy teachers, touchy schoolmates, nosy neighbours, irritating passersby, annoying partners, backward priests, insensitive lovers, ruthless fanatics, corrupt bosses, paranoid dictators and, crossing all the way through the ether of human stupidity, that prevents both its receptors and its transmitters to live happily, I see it reaching all the way up in the sky, brushing past moons, planets and galaxies, getting slightly singed by the tail of a comet, softly poking a spaceship, scratching a black hole, only to arrive, at last, at the private quarters of God, who is startled, mostly because he was certain that such indiscreet intrusions in his personal space had been taken care of after the exemplary punishment of the contractors of Babel, a nasty punishment indeed, turning them into slaves of words, a truly inhumane punishment, but, oh well, he's only a god, not human.

The rest of the members of the holy family gather round the blasphemous member in astonishment. The Son is pulling his dad's mantle, staring at him inquisitively. The Holy Spirit, in the form of a domestic cat, an appropriate disguise for the living room of Paradise, is hissing, its hair standing on end. The Virgin Mary remembers the ever-pointed lily and, red with shame, picks up the china in haste before there are any accidents.

But God is startled for yet another reason. This finger is so familiar, they have met before, he feels as irritated as he did back then, but of course, it's all coming back to him now, the night that old astronomer, somewhere in Italy, was pointing his middle finger towards

102

the skies and God was upset and came down to tell him off, to personally forbid him to point at his private quarters and tamper with the stars and, at last, to teach a lesson to him and all the rest of the smartasses wanting to know everything, even all those things he had specifically told them from the very beginning that they were not allowed to find out. When the old man realised God's presence and listened to his reprimand, he burst out laughing; well, this upset God even more. *You really are an idiot*, said the astronomer in tears. *I am blind, how could I, a blind man, be pointing at the sky?* He roared with laughter, tears rolling down his cheeks, while God, cross-armed wondered how he could punish this already punished, humiliated, imprisoned, and blinded man of blasphemy. He remembered the punishment of Babel, which he always considered as one of his most ingenious ideas.

When the wise man gives the finger, the idiot looks at the moon, the old man giggled. *He who laughs last, laughs longest,* God murmured and quickly teleported himself at some point in the past and the future simultaneously in order to carry out his plan of Galileo's utter annihilation. First he popped into China just to make sure Confucius' words got a little mixed up, then he chopped this disgusting middle finger from Galileo's[19] corpse and made sure it would end up in a glass case in a museum with a poetic inscription clearly stating that the finger

---

[19] Galileo died blind in 1642, after being sentenced to imprisonment in 1633 by the Inquisition due to his heliocentric system theory. In 1737, three fingers, a tooth and a vertebra were stolen from his corpse while it was being moved to the memorial tomb built in his honour at the Santa Croce basilica in Florence. The middle finger is currently on exhibition in room 7 of the Museo Galileo in Florence.

in question is pointing at the stars and heavens. Then he chilled on his ethereal armchair, watching in contentment the divinely prearranged route of things, congratulating himself for yet another invention of words that conceal instead of revealing.

He's now looking at the finger, pointed in the midst of his living room. He's all alone, yet, opposite him, perhaps the only hope of the human race; audacity.

At the goldfish funeral

They play Schubert at the goldfish funeral. *Death and the Maiden*, string quartet nr 14 in d minor. The goldfish was 43 years old[20]. It outlived its initial owners, a couple of pensioners who bought it as a silent companion when their son left home, it lived longer than their son, who died in a car crash at 22, longer than the quartet's Maiden, who has been immortalised (so to speak) by many a painter as a somewhat inappropriately lustful teenager courting with a skinny guy, possibly a chain smoker, and certainly longer than Schubert himself, who died of syphilis when he was 30 years old[21]. But that's life outside the fishbowl for you.

The guests have surrounded the tiny coffin that is being slowly lowered into a gaping, deep hole. Some are wailing, the shyer ones are silently wiping their tears, and others are hiding them beneath their dark glasses. As in all proper funerals, it is drizzling. The moment the coffin touches the bottom of the grave, the quartet starts playing another one

---

[20] The oldest goldfish that has been officially recorded and holds the Guinness record, died at 43 at Yorkshire, England.

[21] Composer Franz Schubert died at 30 of syphilis. Schubert was very shy and rumour has it that he was a virgin until then, that's why his friends bought him a visit to a prostitute from whom he contracted the disease.

of Schubert's great hits, the notorious *Trout*, who roamed the rivers cheerfully only to be captured by a crafty fisherman, in the flower of her youth, before getting a chance to enjoy life in full. But, again, that's life outside the fishbowl for you.

The procession of devastated attendees arrives at the funeral lunch. Before food is served, there will be a reading of excerpts from the goldfish's autobiography in its memory. A woman in black, her eyes red with tears, approaches the stand with a thick book in hand. On the white cover there is a title, *On A Day Like Today*, followed by *BEST SELLER* in red ink. She just stands there, speechless, staring at the open book, turns the page and repeats the same steps several times. The longer she stands there, the louder the wails and sobs of the mourners get. The more she turns the white pages in silence, the more everyone is moved, the more they are overwhelmed with a burning desire to live a life as empty and painless as the life of the deceased goldfish.

By the time she gets to the final page, everyone is lamenting in frenzy, they have fallen on their knees, pulling their hair, praying for a life compiled of todays identical to every other day; without thrills, danger, mishaps, upsetting memories, unfortunate events, peculiar coincidences and inexplicable phenomena. They pray for all their days to be as white as the pages of the autobiography of the goldfish, whose name no one remembers, since not even the goldfish itself could. On their knees, they're begging the spirit of this unsuspecting guru of amnesia to grant them the ultimate relief of every single dawn being an immaculate conception of their selves and every sleep being a womb giving birth to absolute zero. Cameras keep flashing constantly, some of the guests are fainting in ecstasy, others are already feeling the grace of nothingness permeating them, inhabiting them, warming them with charity, so tomorrow morning, on every front page, the prophets of the goldfish will expeditiously lay the foundations of yet another sect, promising the longed-for salvation from the disease of life and its side effects.

It is now time to have lunch, at last. They sit quietly around the long table. Silver cutlery and porcelain dishes are set on the white tablecloth. After this emotional orgy, everyone is starving, looking forward to the food to be served. Needless to say, they are also looking forward to the day when such lowly needs will no longer prevent them from living an exquisitely empty life, yet, for now the hall is flooded with the sound of empty stomachs rumbling in unison. Meanwhile, someone standing at the head of the table is saying grace. *Give us this day, a day like today, every day like every other day.* They all nod with reverence, striving to ignore the tantalizing smell that is making their mouths water. Soon, the waiters arrive and, with a ritually synchronised move, they uncover the soup bowls. Goldfish-soup; their saliva dripping, spreading all the way to the ends of the universe, bathing the trout, enshrouding the vigorous body of a teenager embracing a skinny guy, wetting Schubert's tender heels.

That's life in the fishbowl for you.

The melting of the ice

I can imagine few things more trying to the patience than the long wasted days of
waiting.
On the date fixed for this performance, we were in the midst of a cold snap, but
although the temperature had fallen below -40°, it was decided that the programme
should be carried out as intended.

- Robert Falcon Scott[22]

Nobody's here. Even her cat has left, one morning he simply

walked as far as he could, dug a hole in the snow and stayed in there,

waiting for the blizzard. Her cigarette is burning in the ashtray next

to the sofa, and she's putting her slippers on and off absentmindedly,

feeling the cold on her heels, a palindrome of frost. She's listening

to the blue bougainvillea, growing in murmurs on her pubic mound,

softly pushing beneath her underwear. Then she hears a rub and sees

the shape of a keyhole on the frozen window. Behind the windowpane,

a mouth surrounded by a bunch of facial hair, appears amongst milky

white breaths. And then an eye is peeping at her, fixed on her slippers,

on and off, then it climbs upwards, struggling to sneak under her

---

[22] Robert Falcon Scott (1868-1912), was a British Royal Navy officer who discovered the South
Pole. One of the objects he carried with him in his expedition to the Antarctic was a piano,
frequently played in concerts at the "Royal Terror Theatre", a hut used for the expedition
members' entertainment.

underwear a little indiscreetly.

I brought a toothfish, says Scott softly as he stands at the doorstep.

I wasn't expecting you so early, she replies idly.

Don't get up, I'll put the kettle on and we'll make some fish-soup.

Perfect silence is now collapsing amongst the racket of crockery and cutlery coming from the kitchen. She stands up slowly and gets ready for the piano lesson. She lifts the half dead toothfish, lying on top of the piano, to look for her music scores and then sits down and starts playing.

D Flat Major is like the snow, she says while he's entering the living-room. *It enfolds you quietly until your soul is sweetly frozen.*

Do you believe Chopin had ever seen so much snow in his life?

No idea... Did you ever have any desire to learn the piano before you came to this empty, frozen place? she asks while she keeps playing.

He puts his hand on her pubic mound but doesn't respond. He softly lifts her long skirt and searches beneath her underwear, while she keeps playing expressionlessly. His fingertips find the blue bougainvillea and feel its breath. The more he caresses it the more it grows, it wraps itself around his wrist, his arm, it spreads on her waist, her stomach, her breast and then back to his chest and neck, weaving a blue coat for two around them, four sleeves and a lapel of tender leaves, buds and stalks.

The toothfish is staring at them frozen-eyed as it drips on the music scores. D flat major is breathing with them, contracting and expanding, its peaks frosted, its curves sunken, glistening and sinister, all the shades of white for this portrait of communal silence, a little blue on the edges, perhaps a little melancholy, perhaps a little tedious, yet mating in the south pole has always had a sharp outline. The toothfish will die happy. Right before it became a soup, it witnessed the melting of the ice.

From the lost diary of princess Alexandra of Bavaria[23]

There are not too many truths, there are only a few

- Carl Jung

I have a little glass grand piano in my stomach. The doctor said it's only my impression again. I presume that when he softly parts my curly fringes to kiss me behind my ear, he pretends he cannot hear Ave Maria playing, arpeggios perfectly synchronised with every single circular move of his tongue on my earlobes. This specific piece suits the examination splendidly. The doctor moans and whispers something about lilies and the archangel Gabriel. He says he's the most forgetful angel, that he mixed up the Virgin Mary with Mohamed and that history would have turned out to be really different if an Arab had been impregnated with the saviour of humanity and a woman had written a best seller hundreds of years ago. But, what can you do, shit happens, and it's usually much more crucial than what we bear to believe.

The little glass grand piano in my stomach is crazy for beer. Just a sip of beer is enough to make it start playing waltzes. Dense

---

[23] Princess Alexandra Amalie of Bavaria (1826-1875) suffered from a type of paranoia and believed that she had a miniature glass grand piano in her stomach, which she had swallowed accidentally as a child.

German forests start growing around it and this makes me dyspeptic. There's a bird with a human voice hiding in the forest. But the forest is so dark that no one will ever find it. So much the better for the bird, I'm thinking to myself as I lay with my head high on the velvet fainting couch, trying to digest. I fall asleep and I dream that I'm feeling the darkness with my hands and I find the bird with the human voice. I hold it in my palm as if it were the most precious creature in the world. I open my mouth to speak to it, to tell it not to be scared, that I have no intention to imprison it in a cage but from my mouth comes the voice of a bird, not even a warble but a ghastly squawk. Then the bird starts laughing at me in my face and the more it laughs the more its head resembles a human head. I see the veins on its forehead vibrating violently. I imagine a miniature human brain shivering behind its tiny eyes, struggling to escape from its cranium-shaped cage and then I wake up with a loud burp. I have digested, at last.

The truth is this recurring dream has been on my mind quite a lot because lately I've been experiencing an increasingly similar feeling in my everyday life. The other day, for instance, I was on a train at rush hour. When I find myself in crowded spaces, the little glass grand piano in my stomach starts playing military marches at full volume. As I was standing, crammed between passengers that were visibly annoyed, tired, fed up, hungry, upset, bitter, sleepy, angry and so on, all of a sudden the little glass grand piano burst into a triumphant performance of Elgar's *Land of Hope and Glory*. Within seconds, the crowd of passengers, who, as I mentioned, were already on the verge of fury, lashed out at me, shouting *turn your music down, shame on you, how antisocial, what a dope, turn your phone down, are you fucking deaf*, etc. I tried to explain that I wasn't listening to anything on my phone, that I don't even have a phone because I hate them, that it was the little glass grand piano I had swallowed accidentally when I was little girl but it was all in vain. And of course there was no point in me parting my curly fringes for them to see I wasn't wearing any earphones, as nobody seemed to be listening or paying attention to what I was saying and on top of everything the little glass grand piano was getting ready for its majestic climax right before the grand entrance of the choir.

I elbowed my way out of the carriage at the following stop and walked fast as far as I could from the station. My lace dress was half torn and I felt like crying. I've been sitting on a bench next to the river for hours.

I think of the doctor's peculiar therapy, insisting that it's just my impression, the bird with the human voice, my mother and her damned obsession with glass miniatures. I think of all these things and I'm writing them down in this shabby diary. I'm writing them in order to stop thinking about them. But the more I write about them, the more I think about them so I'd better start writing about something else, perhaps about a misunderstanding, a trivial or serious one, it doesn't matter, shit happens, perhaps I should be writing about a misunderstanding that would be much more crucial than what I'd bear to hope. Someone sits next to me but I don't pay attention to him. He hands me a tissue. A huge cruise ship floats by and stops right in front of us at the pier. *I still have a bit of time, they're waiting for the bridge to be lifted,* says the stranger sitting next to me and I pretend I'm not interested. *Do you play the piano?* he asks and I'm startled. *What makes you say that?* I ask him trying to conceal my agitation. *They're looking for a pianist to play every night at the bar during the cruise,* he replies and I look at him for the first time. *They pay good money,* he adds with an awkward smile. *And of course, accommodation, food and drinks are included. Plus a free holiday on the islands. Only a couple of hours' work every evening.* I wipe my tears with the tissue and I smile back at him. *Yeah, sure I play the piano. Shall we?* He takes me by the hand and we walk towards the pier. *By the way, what do you do on the ship? I mean, are you a crew member or a passenger?* I ask him. *Me? I'm just the piano tuner.*

The Dead & the Fabulous LTD

To find out at last
What sweetness is hidden in the deep for you

- Theocritus, Idyll XI, Cyclops

To attain individuality, we need a large share of death

- Carl Jung

In Rumours Motel, Queen Skyscraper is dreaming of her funeral. Her funeral takes place in the airshaft of a skyscraper. The coffin is lowered with gigantic ropes from the very top, heading slowly towards the open hole. The guests stick their heads out of the windows and as the coffin keeps descending, their tears turn dense like raindrops crashing on the earth, creating little savoury puddles around the grave. Some are holding white handkerchiefs, waving them out of the windows in a farewell gesture. Others are chewing funeral biscuits, swallowing cognac or guzzling hot fish soup noisily. But they're all disguised as skyscraper queens. Their shoulders draped in shawls of stars and fog, while they're scraping the edge of the night sky with their pinkie nails, peeking, turning their noses upwards, searching for the smell of creatures never to be seen.

Queen Skyscraper is suddenly awakened by a light knock on her room's door. *Room service*, an exhausted voice calls out and Queen Skyscraper grants permission to enter. The motel manager, an incredibly elderly man, enters the room slowly pushing a trolley and stops right in front of her bed. On the trailer there are all sorts of foods known to promote longevity. Walnuts, asparagus, berries, dark chocolate, avocado, salmon, coconut oil, broccoli, Brussels sprouts, sauerkraut, kidney beans, green tea, red wine, black coffee, melon, pomegranates, sweet potatoes. Every day, Queen Skyscraper takes one bite and one sip of every single one of those for breakfast.

But today, for the very first time, there is a carton of juice on the trailer that she cannot recognise. The manager informs her that it is mango juice. *It's good for the skin, the hair, the eyes, the digestion, the nervous system, it's even known to be an aphrodisiac*, he says. He himself drinks at least one carton of mango juice per day, *one mango a day keeps the doctor away*, he whispers under his heavy breath. Queen Skyscraper is a little sceptical, she has never tried mango, it never appealed to her, and she always hesitates to try new things. However, the manager insists, so she keeps the carton of mango juice on her bedside table and promises to drink it later. The manager says good morning and leaves the room slowly, followed by a screeching sound that might as well be coming from the trailer or his joints.

Queen Skyscraper decides to watch the rest of her funeral dream. This time, however, she has a feeling that the dream is not hers, that it is not her who is dreaming of it, or rather that she is dreaming of the others dreaming of her funeral. There is a logo on the upper left hand corner of the dream, something like a TV channel logo, *The Dead & The Fabulous LTD*. Also, over the fish-soup sipping soundscape, the sobs and cries, there's a silly music playing now, ramshackle saxophones, nauseating synths and flabby drums, like an 80's soap opera theme tune covering everything in a veil of tawdriness. Queen Skyscraper is lying in the coffin, not wearing her shawl of stars and fog anymore but an outrageous nylon suit with enormous shoulder pads. She's trying to take it off but there's not much space in the coffin and she's pushing the coffin lid with all her might to open it.

And now everyone is gazing at her naked body in the open casket. The soap opera music stops abruptly, spoons are dropping in the fish soup, funeral biscuits remain unchewed, larynxes are scorched by perfectly round gulps of cognac. But Queen Skyscraper is squinting. Since a little girl, she's known that somewhere around her there is a world that escapes her, a world existing as constantly as it escapes her attention. She knows this because every time she squints she manages to steal a peek at tiny snapshots of this world in the vicinity of her peripheral vision.

And she's not Queen Skyscraper there. She is only an egg; a small, white, perfectly shaped egg. All she can feel is her thin shell, a fragile shield containing a secret you may find out only if you break it. Nobody knows what will come out of there. Not even the egg itself. So

121

she doesn't know who she is anymore either.

In the afternoon, when she wakes up at Rumours Motel, she doesn't remember whether she is a crime novel writer, a movie star, an astronaut, a prima donna, a saint, a beekeeper, an archaeologist, a painter, a witch, an astronomer, a conductor, a guru, a terrorist, a swimmer, a dictator, a muse, a vampire, a mermaid, a monster, a piano, a statue, a lovebird, a cat, a sheep, a fish, an aristocrat. She can't even remember if she exists. She only remembers her funeral, which was dreamt by the others whom she saw dreaming of it. She remembers a voice in the egg whispering softly *don't hold on to anything too tight, it will break. Everything breaks.*

Queen Skyscraper is very content. There's nothing as refreshing as not remembering who you are. There's nowhere safer than the tiny void right in the middle of things. This is where you feel as whole as possible. All it takes is to squeeze yourself in there and all of a sudden you become so vast that all innuendos fit inside you without crushing you. Of course, she also can't remember that she doesn't like mango, so she grabs the juice that's left on her nightstand, without thinking twice. Soon, the manager will come to change the sheets and will find her still in bed, with the juice carton in her rigid hand, straw in her half open mouth, eyes turned upwards like the eyes of a stargazer-goldfish[24],

---

[24] The Carassius auratus auratus, also known as "celestial eye" is a mutation of the Stargazer goldfish. The eyes of this goldfish are exceptionally protruding and the pupils are always turned upwards. It initially appeared in China. Its eyesight is quite limited, making it particularly vulnerable to external dangers and also not very competitive compared to other fish when it comes to finding food. They are usually kept in aquariums with other types of fish with limited vision or on their own.

while outside her window, star shaped innuendos will be falling as slow as feathers.

As soon as the motel manager rings the alarm bell, the heads of the rest of the tenants of Rumours Motel appear at the windows. They are all disguised as skyscraper queens, clockwork sighs coming out of their lips. The manager puts a tape in the cassette player and presses play. An 80s soap opera theme tune with ramshackle saxophones, nauseating synths and flabby drums echoes through the entire building. He puts on a pair of surgical gloves and feels the corpse of Queen Skyscraper, calmly and thoroughly, he slips his hands under her clothes, looking for something. In a few moments, he's holding an egg in his hands; a small, white, perfectly shaped egg. He brings it to his lips and softly whispers *don't hold on to anything too tight, it will break, everything breaks.*

He carefully places the egg in his pocket, slowly steps out of the room and locks the door behind him.

Andriana Minou is a musician/writer living in London since 2004. Her work as a writer and poet has been published by *Strange Days Books*, *The Paper Nautilus*, *Rattle Journal*, *FIVE:2:ONE*, *typehouse magazine*, *verbivoracious press*, *poetix*, *Story Brewhouse*, *eyelands*, *Sand Journal*, *tiny spoon*, *Fearsome Critters*, *Maintenant Dada* and more. She has previously published three books with Strange Days Books in Greece. She often presents her books through interdisciplinary performances in various festivals such as Athens European Book Capital, Thessaloniki Queer Arts Festival, Thessaloniki International Book Fair Young Writers' Festival. Since 2015 she has been co-curating Sand Festival, an international literature festival on various beaches of Greece and she is also a judge for Eyelands Book Awards. She is also a founder of the Vladimir&Estragon Piano Duo, Coocoolili and the Oiseaux Bizarres Ensemble. Andriana holds a BA in Piano Performance, an MA in Performing Arts and a PhD in Piano Performance Practice. She has written librettos and performance texts for operas and performances presented around Europe (Amsterdam, Berlin, Athens, New York etc.). As a composer/songwriter, she has released three albums with the DIY label FYTINI (as Delicassetten Machimenai and andrianette) and composed music for various performances and films.

www.andrianaminou.com

Acknowledgements

An Anniversary first published in *Sand Journal* issue 19

The Lernaean Dietrich first published in *Typehouse Magazine* vol. 4, nr. 3, issue 12

Just add water first published in *Tiny Spoon* vol. 2

The Revenge of Cloclo first published at the *Liars' League*

The Dead & the Fabulous LTD first published in *Fearsome Critters* vol. 2

Special thanks to Gregory and Artemis

Made in the USA
Columbia, SC
05 May 2024

35314514R00074